The
Littles
and the Secret Letter

The Littles and the Secret Letter

Adapted by **Teddy Slater**
from *THE LITTLES TAKE A TRIP*
by **John Peterson**
Illustrated by **Jacqueline Rogers**

SCHOLASTIC INC.
New York   Toronto   London   Auckland   Sydney
Mexico City   New Delhi   Hong Kong   Buenos Aires

Tom and Lucy Little watched
Henry Bigg's birthday party
from their secret look-out place.

"I wish we could *really* go to
the party," Lucy said sadly.

"Well, we can't," her brother said.

Tom and Lucy's whole family
lived inside the walls of
Mr. and Mrs. Bigg's house.

There was plenty of room
for them because the Littles
were very, very small.
None of the Biggs even knew
they were there.

"I don't see why we always
have to hide from the Biggs,"
Lucy said. "I want to be friends
with Henry."

"We Littles don't need
to be friends with the Biggs,"
Tom said. "We have each other."

Lucy thought about it.

She could see that Tom was right.

They always had good times

with their family.

Uncle Pete was a great darts player.

Granny Little made the
most wonderful dolls.

And every Sunday night
the whole family played
Go Fish.

And yet . . .

As she looked down at
the party, Lucy wished
for a friend her own age.
"I bet Henry would like me
if he got to know me," she said.

Tom flicked his furry tail.

"Forget it," he said.

"The Biggs must never

know a thing about us.

They might think we are

animals and lock us up

in a zoo."

Lucy's face turned pale.

"Oh, Tom," she cried.

"I did a terrible thing.

I wrote Henry a letter and

put it with his presents—

next to the card I made him."

"Oh, no!" Tom said.

"I've got to get that letter

before Henry reads it."

He ran to the elevator and climbed

inside.

The Littles' elevator was made
from a tin can. It went up and down
between the walls.
Tom rode down
to the living room floor.

Henry and his friends
were playing Pin the Tail
on the Donkey.

So no one saw Tom

scoot across the room.

Tom looked up, up, up

at the Bigg table.

It was covered with

cards and presents.

Hand over hand,

Tom inched his way

up the lamp cord.

It felt like forever

before he reached the top.

Tom climbed onto a gift box
and looked around.
He spotted Lucy's letter
and quickly snatched it up.

But before he could grab
the birthday card, Tom
heard Mrs. Bigg speak.

"There's just enough time to open
the presents before we cut the cake,"
Mrs. Bigg said.
All the children ran to the table
to see Henry's presents.

Tom leaped into a pot of ivy

to hide. He wished he had on

his green shirt instead of the red one.

Someone might see him!

Tom had an idea.

He pulled a green leaf

around him. Now he was safe!

Henry started opening his cards
and presents.

Tom held his breath when
Henry got to Lucy's card.

"It's so tiny," Mrs. Bigg said.

"Who's it from?"

"It's from some girl named Lucy Little,"
Henry said.

"Who's she?" Mrs. Bigg asked.

"I don't know," Henry said.

"Somebody must be playing a joke on me."
He tossed the card aside and
opened the next present.

At last, it was time for the cake.

Henry and his friends went into the kitchen.

This was Tom's chance to get away!

Lucy was waiting when Tom
stepped out of the elevator.
"You got my letter," she said.
"You saved us!"

Together, Tom and Lucy
tore up the letter.
Then Lucy gave her
big brother a big hug.

"I still wish we had some
other children to play with,"
Lucy told Tom.
"But I know I'll never find
a better friend than you!"